I0760653

Short Stories

By Paul O'Grady

Paperback: 978-1-967820-25-2
Hardcover: 978-1-967820-33-7
eBook: 978-1-967820-26-9
Library of Congress Control Number: 2025908305

This is a work of fiction.

Ordering Information:

Prime Seven Media
518 Landmann St.
Tomah City, WI 54660

Printed in the United States of America

TABLE OF CONTENTS

THE BUS RIDE

Being an avid fan of the more private mode of transportation I find the thought of having to take public transport an inconvenience of the highest order and an exercise to be avoided at all costs. Well……..nearly all costs. Sometimes the universe deems it appropriate to test us by putting us in situations that are somewhat out of our control just to see what happens. I'm sure the universe must be run by a woman. (no offence intended) But that's another story. A time not long past falls into this category.

I'm standing outside the garage where my car is booked in to be serviced, waiting for my organized lift to arrive, and my mobile phone rings. "Sorry, got called to a meeting. Won't be able to pick you up. You'll have to take the bus"

These last three words on the text message were like a foreign language to me. "Take the bus ?"………I couldn't recall being on a bus since my school days. The fact that there is a bus stop right out side my house has never kindled the slightest thought of ever actually getting on one. But on this occasion it may be less of an inconvenience than usual. Surely I would be able to manage the walk down my driveway just this once. So bravely I made my way across the road to the bus stop. Twenty or so minutes later I should be at home having a nice hot cup of coffee. No problem……….well almost.

The bus arrives, I climb on board, and, looking around, take the only seat that is available. The aisle seat, perched above the rear axle, next to an old lady who's face had so many wrinkles it could hold a five-day rain. Now. Most modern buses have some system of hydraulic suspension and dampening devices that smooth out the ride but this bus must have been built in the days when that sort of technology could only be found in the monthly subscription to Sci-Fi Magazine. Either that, or someone had removed the springs and replaced them with irregular lengths of forged metal cut from steel girders. Every time we went over a bump I swear I could hear the old lady's dentures rattling. It would start with a slight separation of the buttocks from the seat, then as you came back down, the seat would rise to meet you, smacking you right in the arse, sending you a few inches higher, then as you came back down again it would give you another firm jolt in the behind for good measure. Then everything would settle back down again. All this accompanied by the incessant vibrations of a vehicle that needed the serious attention of a rather strong man with a large spanner. This would happen in nano seconds and be repeated several times in a row. Depending, of course, on the condition of the road and the speed of the bus. The effect this has on the nether regions was two-fold and both at opposite ends of the pain/pleasure spectrum. Firstly, it caused a numbing sensation in the buttocks with isolated patches of acute pain that traveled upwards along the spine visiting every single vertebrae and nerve ending, and secondly, and more interestingly, all this bumping and vibrations traveling through the seat tended to arouse the 'little fella' sleeping down below. He'd be aroused from his sleep. Not fully awake, but enough to realise that something was happening. The same way a sleeping dog will raise it's head, have a bit of a look around, then flop back down again. Except this thing never flopped back down.

Now this is, to a large extent, controllable. You look out the window, try to focus on something of interest, sing a song to yourself or go over an imaginary shopping list in your mind. Anything to take your mind off the problem and usually it will go away. Another bump, more vibrations. You move around and fidget a bit. Another bump……..a little bit more awake………you look out the window again…………more vibrations…………you start to talk to a total stranger hoping that meaningless conversation will take your mind off the ever expanding problem.

More bumps, more vibrations. More awake. Now a keen eye would probably make out that something wasn't quite right. Another series of bumps and you squirm around in your seat trying in vain to find a comfortable spot for him to just lay down and go to sleep. Bump. …..Bump. If you're wearing a pullover, this is the time to try and pull it over the problem area in an attempt to disguise it from curious eyes. More vibrations………… And just when you think things can't get any worse, up ahead you see it. Getting closer by the second. Directly in the path of the bus…………the East Side railway crossing. Six lines. Twelve solid metal railway tracks. Potholes in the bitumen between each track surrounded by bumps and lumps that have been formed over time by an endless trail of heavy vehicles. You try and will the bus driver to slow down but no. He seems to know exactly what he is doing. Like he's been taught the equation. That magical mathematical equation drummed into him by some twisted facilitator at Bus Drivers School. The simple yet effective equation………… Train tracks plus rear axle seat vibrations multiplied by speed over prolonged time equals one raging, blood engorged erection.

By the time we exited the other side I was wearing a pair of shorts that more resembled a four-man tent. You can try and hide it but you will be doomed to failure. Short of jamming a cold spoon down my pants I am left helpless. In natures hands, so to speak. The bell rings. On the roof at the front of the bus a light starts to flash. 'Next Stop'. Next to me the old lady starts to gather her bags and begins to stand. My god. The fat old bag will have to squeeze past me. Shit. I pray to the flaccid Gods to turn her blind lest she sees the raging monster before her. She squeezes past me. I close my eyes….waiting for the scream…….She seems totally oblivious to it. She moves past me. Never flinching. Thank Christ she hasn't spotted it. I begin to relax a bit. The bus slows down and pulls in towards the curb. Relaxed for the moment but still at full mast, I peer out the window and my worst nightmare unfolds before my eyes. Waiting to board the bus are more than two dozen giggling, high-school girls. Frantically I look around for a spare seat up the back. None. I think about getting off (the bus that is) but it is too late. They are already piling on and moving down the aisle towards me. The only spare seat is next to me. I look down and the beast is now fully awake and starting to poke his head out for a look to see what all the mental commotion is about. I close my eyes and curse my self for not taking my mothers advice all those years ago. "Always make sure you have clean underwear on when you go out" she would often say to me. Right now I would settle for *any* underwear. Even an old soiled pair of 'Y' fronts. Inside I was going into a slow-burn panic. Do I stand up and give them the seat? Exposing my manhood to the world? No. Do I try and hide it from view as I rush for the exit door? Would that only draw attention to myself? Probably. I turn as sideways as I possibly can and attempt to take up both seats. Rude and ignorant male chauvinist pig? Yes. I can live with that for the moment. The lesser of three evils.

Talking and giggling, they slowly edge their way towards me. I try not to look. I try to think of something as far removed from having an erection as you can possibly get. Old nuns and dead kittens. THAT'S IT… I'll think about OLD NUNS AND DEAD KITTENS. In my mind. Over and over. I think of old nuns and dead kittens.
The bus jerks and moves away from the stop. Another pothole……… old nuns……The girls move closer…………dead kittens. The bus gathers speed……..old nuns……..and hits another pothole………. dead kittens. My mind is filling up with old women in black full length habits and squashed small furry animals. The next stop approaches…………old nuns……….The bus moves towards the curb……….dead kittens……….old nuns and dead kittens. No luck. He's still there. Looking around the bus. I just hope he doesn't see the high-school girls. And then disaster struck. As the bus pulled into the curb…another pothole. This time with just enough geometry, bounce

and angle to unbalance one of the girls and like a domino effect in slow motion, she falls into her friend, who falls into another and like the small silver metal balls that swing from their strings suspended in a line in their frame........one into the next, into the next.....I know that the last one will react to the inertia exerted upon it and have nothing to spend it's kinetic energy on except.......................me.

As she lands bum first in my lap, skirt flying up around her hips, I scream the first thing that comes into my mind............DEAD FUCKING KITTENS !
I desperately try to push her off by grabbing her on the hips. Unfortunately she has already been informally introduced to my little friend and tries vainly to get up. My scream is followed closely by hers.............HE"S GOT HIS DICK OUT. Now. Innocent as it may be, I must admit that from a distance it could be considered to be something far worse than what it actually was. Me with my hands on her hips, pushing and shoving, and my member bouncing around untethered and her writhing around screaming and yelling. From a distance it would look suspicious to say the least. And that distance you ask?. Well. It is the exact distance from my seat to the bus driver. I finally get her off me and begin to push my way past the hordes of screaming girls. Still fully erect I might add. The driver sees me making a 'B' line for the side door and in an heroic attempt to keep the molester onboard, decides to shut the doors. I see the doors start to close. I turn sideways and lunge for freedom between the rapidly closing doors. And freedom would have been mine except for one rather large detail. A fully erect penis. He is battered against

the door frame as I squeeze out the gap. I fall onto the footpath in a crumpled heap. Agony. I can see the front doors open and the bus driver leaps off the bottom step. I have no choice but to get to my feet and try to run. My sorry old penis has beaten a hasty retreat. Hunched over like a crippled madman I run. Holding my hands over my throbbing, battle scarred penis. Around the corner and finally to safety. A description that, no doubt will quickly be relayed to the nearest policeman.

It took several days to heal the physical damage to the little fella. It will probably take several years to heal the mental anguish. And as for the poor schoolgirl? Well, I can only hope that she makes a full recovery and doesn't harbor any grudges against mankind.

And as for bus rides? I only take taxi's these days. And if I see a railway crossing ahead? I tap the driver on the shoulder and say…….
"Next left please"

THE END

THE CALL

A Short Detective Story, by a Short Detective

Waiting was never on of my strongest virtues. When it came to waiting I had about as much patience as a VD Clinic doctor in the Virgin Islands and here I was, sitting in the run down office of my detective agency for hours waiting for the phone to ring. Waiting for one very special phone call. Everything that I'd worked for over the last thirty-seven years was about to come to fruition. All I had to do was wait for the call. If the call didn't come it would be back to life as usual. Back to the daily grind of endless, meaningless jobs. Back to the constant throbbing behind the eyes brought on by having to listen to too many whining old farts with nothing better to do than try to screw me down for less money to do their shitty little surveillance work. Waiting. Staring at the phone and waiting. They had assured me that the call would be coming. But I had to be here to take it. There was no second chance. Nothing and no one was going to get in the way of this call. Waiting. It was now only a matter of time.

The day was dragging like a fat mans clubfoot and here I was, hunched over the phone like a half shut suitcase. Waiting. I could hear the second hand on the clock pounding in my brain like a relentless jackhammer on Valium. And still I waited.

The frigid wind whistling through the 38mm semi-automatic bullet holes in the window behind my desk would have made a polar bear homesick. Home. That's where I wish I was right now. Home. Spooning some leggy blond under a duck-down quilt in front of a roaring fire. Stopping just long enough to let the love tide ebb and down a snifter or two of Louis XIV cognac before re-engaging in some unrestrained feral activities. Home. My mind wondered back to the leggy blond. Over her toned and tanned legs, up and around her taut and femininely muscular thighs, went for a dip in her sweat filled navel before scaling the eastern side of her 44 triple D alps.

The phone rang and snapped my mind back to reality like a ten-dollar hooker removing a G-string wedgie from her chubby fat arse. Was this to be the call that I'd been waiting for?

The phone played its duo-tone melody once more. Was this to be the call that would change my life forever? Was this the once-in-a-lifetime opportunity that was going to take me off the crappy sideshow merry-go-round of this mundane existence?

The phone rang once more. Should I take the change, knowing full well that once I answered the call there would be no turning back. Ever. I sucked a bead of sweat from the top of my lip as my trembling hand reached towards the receiver. The phone rang one more time.

I hesitated. A thousand thoughts flashed through my mind. Should I or shouldn't I. Is it worth risking everything for that one throw of the dice?

My fingertips touched the handpiece just as the phone rang again. I pulled back in fright and hesitated for a second then cautiously reached for the phone again. It was now or never. I knew that if I didn't answer the call soon then the phone would stop ringing forever. Damn the consequences. To hell with reason and conscience. Everyone takes a gamble once in their life. If you don't you never know what might have been. You spend the rest of your miserable, useless life fighting the demons of denial never knowing what really would have happened. Trying to convince yourself that you made the right choice when deep down inside the thought that your whole life could have been quantumly different if only you had decided to grab that chance when it presented its self, eats away at you like crows picking at the carcass of a discarded road kill on the gravel shoulder of life's highway.

The phone rang once more. My hand touched the receiver. A trickle of perspiration ran down the back of my neck, under my collar and slowly down my spine as I slowly squeezed my hand over the handpiece. The tension was palpable. It oozed from every pore. I felt the pit of my stomach slowly twist itself in to a maze of knots.

Slowly I raised the handpiece. Every fibre of my being, every nerve was charged with enough electricity to light Manhattan for a month. My hand started to tremble uncontrollably as I slowly raised the handpiece towards my ear.

I took a deep breath and closed my eyes. This will be a new beginning. This will be the end to the daily grind in this rat infested hovel. No more TV dinners late at night as I sit on the edge of my torn and outdated, flea plagued couch watching re-runs of the re-runs of old black and white episodes of 'My Three Sons'. No more freezing night-time stakeouts watching the fat bottomed wife of some jealous, overweight, lower middle class shoe salesman do the wild thing with some mono-syllabic Hispanic shopping trolley collector from the local Kwiky-Mart only to find that he wants her back and decides to cancel the cheque just before my rent is due.

No more chasing after some underage, love-torn teenage runaway only to have her boyfriend pound the living crap out of me as I try to explain that her father wants her back and I'm only doing my job. No more risking my life to track down some bail-jumping, psycho-crazed Neanderthal who doesn't really care if he dies or who he takes with him.

I know deep down in the bowels of my soul that I'm making the right decision. I know that I could not spend one more nano-second in this god forsaken cesspool of discarded human compost, the sleazy trailer trashed dime-a-day foot slogging thankless den of filth and corruption.

No. Things are going to change. I'm going to make them change. Time to take care of business and look after number one.

As I close my eyes and I can hear the waves crashing onto the sand outside my secluded, three story Cayman Island beachfront villa.

I can smell the delicate aromas of boiling lobster wafting in the twilight breeze from the alfresco restaurant down on the bay.
I can see the bright orange tropical sun as it dips into the evening ocean only to be replaced by a turquoise and crimson sunset that melts up into an azure velvet blanket sky, dotted with millions of shimmering, sparkling diamond stars.
I can feel the gentle yet firm caress of a topless, twenty something island goddess as she slowly massages the tension out of every muscle as I lay under the swaying palms on a balmy summer night.
I can hear the incessant beep…beep…beep of a dead phone line after someone has hung up the receiver.
Oh FUCK ! ……..

Oh FUCKIN"HELL !

NOOOOOO !

FARRRRRRRRRRKKKK !

I gently slammed the phone down and watched it shatter into a million tiny plastic shards.

Silence.

Deathly, complete and absolute silence.
It was a silence as black and foreboding as looking into the grim reapers hollow eyes just before his scythe cuts its lazy path through your soul.

Silence

I sit and look at the lopsided remains of the telephone on the desk in front of me. My mind and face blank. An ocean of total helplessness washes uncontrollably over me. Deep primal urges race to the surface and spread through my numbing body.

I undo the clip on my shoulder holster and retract my revolver. Staring at the deformed telephone I slowly raise the muzzle and rest it against the underside of my chin.

I squeeze the trigger.
I can feel nothing.
Less than nothing.
Total blackness.
Silence

The hollow echo of the gunshot finds it's way through the cracks in the wall and as the last echoes fade out, the growing silence is shattered by a familiar sound. It is the deformed ring of a blood splattered telephone sitting lopsidedly on the floor.

They decided to ring back.

THE END

THE LONGEST DAY

The Past

My name is Robert and this is my story. The story of what turned out to be my longest day.

Sometimes it can seem like every day is the longest day.

When Jacquie came into my life just over six years ago I could never have imagined what changes were about to take place. From the moment we met things were different. She was bright and bubbly and a bundle of energy. As our eyes met for the first time I could tell, instantly, that she loved me and from that moment I knew that I loved her and that we would always be part of each other's life. I loved her more than I had ever loved a living thing before. It was also the moment that changed forever my life with Chesna, my wife for the past nine years.

To understand why, you need to go back a few years. Back to when things between my wife and myself were at their best. Back to a time when we didn't have the stresses and problems that plague most relationships at some stage. Back to her upbringing to see the things that shaped her into the person she became.

Chesna was the younger of two girls born to third generation Polish immigrants. Her name is Slavic for peaceful. An irony reflected by her life. At the tender age of five her father died of liver disease after a lifetime of alcohol abuse. She told me once that he never got over the memory of seeing his grandparents dragged away from their home by Nazi soldiers. He had been living with them ever since his parents were killed in a car accident when he was only ten years old.

She said it haunted him night and day. Haunted him to his grave. Her mother did her best to bring up both girls but lacking the discipline of a father figure her sister, Hannah, older by three years, ran away when Chesna was only thirteen. They never heard from her again.

This broke her mothers heart and after years of living with the guilt that she should have done more to hold the family together, the grief, eating away inside her, finally took it's toll and on 11th May 1984, on what would have been Hannah's 21st birthday, her mother took her own life.

Eighteen years old, with a handful of possessions, no family and few friends, she found herself on her own. She moved into a two-bedroom unit with an elderly lady that had befriended the family some years before.

With just a basic education and no work experience there was little opportunity to do anything apart form meaningless factory work. But she always had a smile on her face. It's as if she knew that one-day things would get better and when they did she would be ready to greet that moment with a beaming, happy smile that no amount of past pain could diminish.

That smile was her key to happiness. It radiated a warmth that was almost tangible. It was the first thing that everyone noticed about her. Notable considering her long ringlets of auburn hair and her creamy cover girl complexion would have most models flying into a jealous rage.

It was as if she didn't know how *not* to smile. It was a smile that could win friends instantly and disarm the most hostile personality with just a flash of her ivory white teeth. Yet it wasn't a false smile. It was an honest smile. As natural as her personality. A smile that immediately put you at ease.

And it was that smile that caught my eye one winters night at the local tavern.

2

The Meeting

Chesna had just turned twenty-three and was out having a few drinks with friends and I was one year older and studying law at the state university.

Looking back it seems that fate had thrown us together because like Chesna, I too had lost both parents before my twentieth birthday. Since then I had been living between a spare room at my aunt's place and a university campus dorm. I had decided to put most of my social life on hold so that I could concentrate all my energies on my studies. Romantic thoughts of women were far from my mind as I sat on the verandah of the tavern celebrating a friend's birthday on that cold evening.

Someone decided that it was my turn to buy the next round of drinks so obligingly I made my way through the crowd to the bar inside.

And there, as I glanced around at the faces waiting to be served, I saw the most beautiful woman that I could ever have imagined. Our eyes arced around the room, sweeping closer with each second until the arcs crossed. At the time I swore that for the briefest of moments our eyes held each other's gaze. I was captivated and I imagined that she too must have felt the same. I could see it in her smile. The way that the corners of her mouth curled upwards just a little. as our eyes met and then held that position as her eyes continued on their slow arc across the room.

It wasn't until years later, when talking about that first night that she finally admitted that she did notice me that night, at that exact moment that our eyes met. It was a truth that I had known in my heart from that moment on.

By the end of winter we were close friends and by summer we were in love. Deferring my studies for a year we went to Europe for a 6 months hiking holiday. We started in England, then crossing the channel into France, worked our way through the southern provinces until, finally we found ourselves in Poland. It was Chesna's wish to try and locate any living relatives that might still be there. Although we tried every authority and government department we hit a dead-end at every turn. I suggested that we go to the sites of the concentration camps to see if there was a mention of her relatives on any of the memorials thinking that it might be a starting point but that too proved fruitless. We were unable to find any living relatives anywhere on this earth. But she never lost her smile. Never.

A couple of years later, with a gathering of close friends in a beautiful garden setting, we were married. It was the happiest day of our lives. It seemed that all of the bad karma from her childhood was finally erased with the promise of a new life together. To be able to start our own little piece of history. A new beginning. It seemed only natural to want to start our own family.

Within two years I had graduated with honors and had joined a flourishing law firm. Chesna was doing part-time work at a craft shop and her natural artistic ability was starting to shine through. We were deeply in love. The kind of all encompassing love that surrounds you like a warm blanket on a winter's night.

It was one of those winters night when we were celebrating the fourth anniversary of our meeting that we finally decided to try and start a family. We had talked about it several times an although be both agreed that it would be a beautiful way to express our love for each other we never got around to setting a timeframe. But there is something about a warm bed on a cold night. We often found it to be the perfect aphrodisiac for romance. And this night was no exception.

Over the next twelve months we kept trying but our efforts, apart from being wonderful lovemaking experiences were fruitless when it came to getting Chesna pregnant. We both started to blame each other and then ourselves. It seemed that a chink in our protective emotional armor had appeared. We could have decided to keep blaming ourselves and spiral out of control but we both needed each other far too much to ever let that happen. We sought specialist advice, went through countless tests and finally started on the IVF program.

Although the doctors and nurses involved were wonderful people and they did their best to reassure us that everything would be ok, in the end it seemed that we would never be able to have children.

We spent two and a half years trying different diets, positions, times and endless tests but nothing gave even the slightest glimmer of hope. So it came as a total shot from the blue the morning that Chesna came in to tell me that she thought that she might be pregnant. We both sat on the edge of the bed, held each other and cried.

Further tests confirmed that Chesna was indeed very much pregnant. Just as the doctors couldn't explain why it wouldn't happen they had just as much trouble trying to figure out why it suddenly did.

We weren't concerned with the whys and wherefores we were just happy that it finally happened. It is said that quite often, after couples give up trying and the stress levels decrease, they inexplicably fall pregnant. This may have been the case.

Suddenly all of our priorities changed. There was a nursery to paint, clothes and appliances to buy and of course a room full of stuffed toys collect. We were happy, in love and about to give birth to our first child. Or so we thought.

3

The Agony

There is something about a woman carrying a child inside them that gives them a bloom in their appearance that nothing on this earth can match. It almost defies description. It is a radiance that burns bright from within and extends out to touch everyone around them. Even total strangers. People walking down the street. Consumed with their own world and all it's problems are suddenly touched by it's candescence. They can ask the most personal questions and reach out and touch the swollen belly of a total stranger without the slightest hint of embarrassment. It draws them into your world for a brief moment and as they depart you are sure that their world will be a better place, no matter how briefly, for having stopped and been touched by the light. Add to this Chesna's irrepressible smile and you have the recipe to heal the world.

Chesna kept working at the craft shop. She found it both therapeutic and beneficial because she was able to keep busy through the troubled times and make all sorts of baby things for the upcoming birth. We often talked about when she should give the work up but she refused to even slow down. She figured that she would know when it was time to take a rest. Still, her collapse came as a complete and devastating shock to us all.

I received the call at work. Helen, who owned the shop, said that Chesna was taken to the county hospital after becoming dizzy and fainting. I assumed that she was pushing herself too hard and had over exerted herself. I arrived at the hospital twenty minutes later and was informed that she was in a stable condition and that the baby was fine. They wanted to keep her over night for observation. Just to make sure all was well. We held hands and cried and hugged each other and cried some more. It was a numbing feeling seeing my wife lying in a hospital bed hooked up to a monitor. It was to become an all too familiar sight over the next few months. One that I would never get use to.

Chesna was discharged the next day with explicit instructions to take it easy. She took this as her body telling her that it was time to take a rest. She resigned from the craft shop and set her energies to preparing the house for the upcoming event. Although she was taking it easy she always seemed tired. We didn't think it was anything out of the ordinary. She was seven and a half months into the pregnancy and it seemed quite normal to be tired.

Waking up to a pregnant woman screaming in pain is a sobering experience. She was still six weeks short of full term yet it seemed like she was going into labour. We rushed to the hospital and she was admitted straight away. Her obstetrician assured us that it was nothing to worry about but two hours later she was rushed in for an emergency caesarian. The baby had stopped omitting any signs of life. I was numb with fear. For Chesna and the baby.

Being present while the doctor delivered our stillborn baby was the single most emotion retching moment of my life. Words fail to describe the feelings churning up inside. It's as if your heart has been torn out of your chest and theirs nothing left but an empty hollow void. Nothing prepares you for it and nothing can ease the pain. Nothing. Chesna could see the hurt in my eyes. We cried for so long that I thought we would both drown in the tears. At times it seemed like I could easily just slip into the ocean and not come up. But there was more to come.

During the C-section the doctors discovered that Chesna had ovarian cancer. She must have been in great pain but she never let on. She never stopped smiling.

The next few months were consumed by panic, pain, constant worry, chemotherapy sessions and the grief of losing our first child. At the time of birth we hadn't chosen a name. But we decided to call her Shahla. In Afghani it means beautiful eyes.

4

The Last Days

They say that the Lord moves in mysterious ways. Some might even say twisted. Because amongst all the confusion and against all the odds another miracle occurred. Chesna fell pregnant again. It was so unexpected. We were busy trying to save one life and inside we created another. It was hard for me to tell if it was for the best or some macabre trick played on us by a higher being with a warped sense of reality. But Chesna decided that this time it would all work out. And who was I to argue with a pregnant woman. She knew it would be difficult and the doctors tried to talk her out of it. They suggested an abortion but neither of us could bare the thought of losing another child and that is the way we thought of the tiny baby inside. It was our child. They told her of the dangers involved with the chemotherapy, so she decided to stop chemo to give the baby every chance to survive. She was, in effect, giving her life for the unborn baby's.

As the months passed Chesna became visibly weaker. She became drawn and pale and was in constant pain. But she always had a smile on her face. Sometimes it had to fight its way past the pain that was racking her body and mind but it was always there. Always. The words awe inspiring would not even begin to describe the feeling of pride that I had for her. Yet I would have done anything to change places with her. It didn't seem fair.

We never talked about what seem inevitable. It was just something that was silently understood between us. She could see how I was hurting and she comforted and reassured me. I drew my strength from her. At times I felt guilty for it. I thought that I should have been stronger. I felt totally useless. It was out of my hands. It was in the lap of some twisted god and I knew that he would be anything but kind.

The doctors told us that the best way would be to do a C-section at the earliest opportunity. They wanted to take the baby out at 35 weeks to give Chesna the best chance of recovery but once again she refused their request. She wanted to go as close to full term as possible to give the baby every chance of survival. I was torn between two impossible decisions and found that, in the end, I had to grant her wish.

The final weeks were horrendous for her. She was in constant pain but refused all but the most harmless drugs. Her commitment and unconditional love for that unborn child was exceptional and at times, I thought, bordered on insane. I could understand why she would sacrifice her life for the baby's but I found it increasingly harder to understand how she could sacrifice her life with me. There were times, I'll admit, that I felt selfish. But it only took a flash of her smile to humble me back to reality.

The doctors warned her against having a natural birth. They insisted that a C-section delivery would be much safer but Chesna had a strong will and nothing was going to stop her experiencing the only birth she was ever likely to have. As much as I wanted to side with the doctors I had to support her dying wish. The labour was long and painful. But it was hard not to be inspired by her iron will and determination. Chesna had started having contractions in the early hours of the morning. Just after midnight. And now it was nearly ten thirty at night. It was the longest day of our life.

At six minutes to midnight and with one final, agonizing push the baby came into this world. Chesna opened her eyes and wiped back the tears as she reached out and touched the newborn child. And as the smile slowly slipped from her face Chesna slowly faded from our mortal lives.

I looked down at the crib and our eyes met. She was bright and bubbly and I loved her from the moment that I saw her. Our daughter Jacqui. A shock of auburn hair and her mothers smile.

I looked back at my wife. Lying motionless on the hospital bed.
Chesna.
Slavic for peaceful.

We named our daughter, Jacqui after Chesna's mother.

It was the happiest, saddest day.

Six years later and she is still the love of my life. She always will be. She knows the sacrifice that her mother made so that she would survive and not a day goes by that we don't remember the love she had for her.

Our beautiful daughter, Jacqui

THE END

THE THIRD MISTAKE

(or…no nose is good nose)

Everyone knows that there are basic differences between men and women. Biological, sexual, spiritual and ……mental. One of the least understood (by women anyway) is the changes that take place when our immune systems is invaded by the dreaded lurgy. That's right. When women get sick they are ….well……just sick. But when us men get sick we are dying. We die a thousand deaths in our lifetime. Women just don't understand the suffering that we have to go through every time the flu or a severe cold gets its death grip on our souls. The endless aching, the constant pain and agony that we have to endure. We try to hide it from them but in the end the level of pain can be so great that in our weakened state we let our guard slip and from the discomfort of our death bed, cry out in torment for their facilitation and compassion. Well that's what I told my wife one morning when I woke in the early hours with a lethal bout of sinusitis. Her reply was short and swift. "Stop your complaining and go and take something for it". After which she promptly returned to sleep.

They say that things come in threes. It can be said that this is also true of mistakes. I dragged my weary body in the semi-darkness down the hallway to the kitchen. Edging around the table and chairs I located the medicine cabinet where I had recently noticed an open packet of SINUTAB. Now. Having built the medicine cabinet during the daytime I could see no need to fit a light inside. Mistake number one.

Groping around in the semi-light I grabbed the packet and popped two tablets from the open satchel. Just as I was about to close the door I decided that it would be a good idea to take the other, full satchel to work with me in the morning just in case. Mistake number two.

My head throbbed all through the morning meetings and by the time I stopped for lunch it had a firm hold of me. It was in the transition from acute to chronic maxillary sinusitis. It felt like somebody had stood me on my head and filled my nasal cavities with a mixture of crazy putty and super glue. You couldn't get to my adenoids with a jackhammer. Solution?...pop another couple of tabs. That should fix it.

Afternoon tea time and still no relief. Solution?...Pop some more tabs. It's a male thing. We never follow recipes when we cook, we have a primal need to assemble intricate and complicated equipment without the need for instructions and when it comes to medications we prefer to go by the dosage that we feel we need rather than what may be written on some silly directions that are only intended for children and the aged and infirmed. We men know better. Or do we?

I took another two tablets before retiring early that night. The sinus was still there and now I had the onset of stomach cramps to contend with. I woke up again in the early hours with severe diarrhoea. A quick trip to the toilet and........two more tabs. I returned to bed and slept fitfully until the alarm rattled me awake around 7am. I had to go to work. There were project deadlines to meet. I had no choice. A cup of coffee, a slice of toast and two tabs later I was on my way to the office. I spent most of the morning rushing between my office and the toilets. Talk about deadlines.

The diarrhoea was getting worse and the sinus wasn't getting any better. I couldn't stomach any lunch so I washed down the last two tablets with a mild latte and headed home early. I was really dying now. Just to make me feel better, my devoted and caring wife had replaced her "Stop your complaining and go and take something for it" with "Stop your complaining and go see a doctor"

Humbly I rang and made an appointment for the following day. Now I had full-blown fatal sinusitis. I could feel myself slowly slipping away. My face felt like an over-inflated soccer ball, my stomach felt like someone was slowly tightening a vice around my lower intestines and my ass was red raw and burning from the constant attention it was receiving. I was at deaths door and I could hear it creaking open.

I had used the entire satchel that I'd taken to work and so I made my way back to the medicine cabinet. I knew that there were only a couple of tablets left in the opened satchel so it was with some surprise that I found the SINUTAB packet nearly full. There were only a couple missing from the satchel and the other was unopened. I scratched my head in puzzlement. It didn't make any sense. That is until I found a similar packet opened and sitting next to the SINUTAB. I slowly removed the packet from the shelf and flipped open the lid. Inside I found one satchel. It only had two tabs left and the other satchel was missing. I held the packet to the light so that I could get a better look. It read SENETAB. A natural herbal laxative.

"Honey" I called to my wife, "I think I found the problem".
Mistake number three

THE END

TRAPPED WITHIN

CHAPTER 1

The winter sun fingered its rays over the tops of the blue gums and pushed its way past the half-open drapes. Playing angular shadows, like silhouetted marionettes, over my eyelids.

I was awake before I was even aware. The irrepressible sunlight trying to lever open my eyes and force me to face another day. Taunting me with its cheerful salutations.

Like a market stall owner pulling down his awning at the first sign of rain, I try to close my eyes and block out the light only to realise that they are already closed. Even though the daylight heralds newer, brighter beginnings, deep in my tortured black heart, the heart that once overflowed with so much love was slowly filling with sulphurous rain from the emotional storm that hammered at the door of my soul. And rattled the very foundations that supported my weathered and frail sanity.

A hollow man. That is all that I have become. Just an empty shell. All meaning, all emotion all semblance of any living entities, gone. Within these walls that, on the outside, showed little difference to the person I once was, there now dwelt lonely shadows of despair, the ghosts of regret and the remnant dust of love long vanished.
Imprints of life without any life of their own. A fool's memories.

CHAPTER 2

The calendar showed a different day, a different year, but for all the things that changed outside my bitter world, within, everything remained the same.
The same year, the same day and time. Nothing changed. Twelve minutes past three in the morning. Sunday the 17th of November 2011.
That's where I was trapped.
Eternality running from the same demons.

Occasionally I could find a dark corner to hide in. A refuge.
Crouched there in the blackness I can hear them approaching. I can smell their indifference and as they creep closer I can feel their hot, waxy breath.
Slowly a finger curls around the edge of my mental sanctuary, followed by another.
I cower from them. From the demons of my past.
Their sharp nails claw at my memory. Incessantly gouging new wounds in my mind.

Like tendrils, arching around me and dragging me back to reality.

Some days I pray that I will go mad to escape the crushing weight of the demons that haunt me.
Other days I find myself clutching at my last threads of sanity as they drag me down into the abyss. But most days I just lay here waiting for my final breath to depart.

I don't wait for death because I'm already dead. After years of denouncing the religious beliefs from my youth, I finally realise that there is a hell.
I'm living this hell every day. It's inescapable.
For as long as I am alive I am dead.
Only when I finally die will I be released from its torment.

CHAPTER 3

A nurse enters the room. I can hear her humming as she moves around the bed to open the drapes.
"Good morning William. Did you sleep well? It's a beautiful day outside".
If only she knew how much I hate that trite, well-meaning bullshit.
Does she have any idea how tormenting it is to have someone be so condescending?
As if I give a fuck about the weather.
And I hate it when she opens the drapes in the morning.

Can't she realise that I'm trying to hide from the light?
And I hate that fucking tune that she is always humming.

I lay here imagining ways to kill her. To stop the torment. I try to get into her mind.

Maybe I can control her. Make her walk straight out the door and under a bus.
I concentrate with all my will power but nothing ever happens. Nothing.
The humming continues and fades into the distance as the nurse leaves the Intensive Care Unit. I.C.U. The contradiction is not lost on me.

I.C.U. But I cannot see you. Just as you can't really see me.
All I can see is the light bleeding through my semi-opaque eyelids. Images dancing. Colors flickering, forming nameless shapes then morphing into other shapes within themselves.

Shapes that remind me of the past. Shapes and memories that drift randomly through my mind.
Backsliding. Cascading. Reforming into the ugly images of that night.

I can smell the demon's acrid breath as they approach. I try to chase them back into the cracks of my conscience but they split into ribbons of fervid dementia and engulf me.

Clawing and pawing at me with their razor sharp pincers.
Each slash tearing away another protective layer until it lies in tatters.

Exposing the hidden truths that I keep locked away.
The truths of the 17th of November.

They scratch at the layers of denial. The stratum of lies.
Lifting. Peeling. Exposing.

In my mind I try to run from them but my feet are like lead.
I try to hide but each shelter evaporates, leaving me exposed to the pursuing demons.
I try to bury them in my sub-conscience.
But like skeletons in a flooded crypt they rise to the surface in all their horror.
And with a twisted grin on their lopsided heads, they tease me into remembering.
Truths.
Forcing me to recall in all it's horrific, vivid color, every fateful event.
The party. The drinking. The argument. The crying kids in the back seat.
The road. The speed. The curve. The tree.

The slow implosion of contorted and gnarled metal. The shattered glass, exploding into me, through me.
I can hear the bolts shearing off as the sudden deceleration imparts unbelievable pressure on the occupants of this compacting tomb.
I can hear the garbled dying cries of my own family.
I can hear the vacuumous sounds of their departing souls leaving their bodies, one by one.

I wait for my turn but it never comes.
I lay trapped. Entombed within myself.
A prison without shape or form but with invisible walls as strong and impenetrable as any man-made fortress.

CHAPTER 4

Day fades into twilight.
The sunlight is replaced by the candesence of the overhead florescent tubes.
Unnatural light forming unnatural images in my minds eye.
Images. Thoughts. Memories.
Demons.

Fitful sleep finally comes.
How long did I sleep before the sunlight woke me? I do not know.

Time is irrelevant now.
My constant heartbeat my only companion until the demons return.

The cycle continues.

Trapped within.

THE END

www.ingramcontent.com/pod-product-compliance
Lightning Source LLC
Chambersburg PA
CBHW030416310726
48979CB00002B/433

* 9 7 8 1 9 6 7 8 2 0 3 3 7 *